This copy of

A Book of Cats

belongs to

H. Novels

Also available by the same authors

A Book of Pig Tales
A Book of Bears

and by David McKee with Katie Wales

A Book of Elephants

A BOOK OF CATS

Compiled by Rosemary Debnam

Illustrated by David McKee

BEAVER BOOKS

A Beaver Book
Published by Arrow Books Limited
62-5 Chandos Place, London WC2N 4NW

An imprint of Century Hutchinson Ltd

London Melbourne Sydney Auckland
Johannesburg and agencies throughout the world

First published by Kaye and Ward 1983

Beaver edition 1987

Illustrations © David McKee 1983 and 1987

Set in Janson
by WBC Print Ltd, Bristol

Made and printed in Great Britain
by The Guernsey Press Co. Ltd.,
Guernsey, C.I.

ISBN 0 09 954820 8

Contents

The publishers are grateful to the following for permission to use copyright material in the English edition of this book: Dennis Dobson for *I'm Not Frightened of Pussy Cats* from SILLY VERSE FOR KIDS by Spike Milligan © 1959 Spike Milligan; Ursula Moray Williams for *Gobbolino's Hallowe'en* © 1983 Ursula Moray Williams; Chatto and Windus for *The Cat and the Mouse* from THE WONDER DOG by Richard Hughes; Margaret Mayo for *Why the Manx Cat Has No Tail* and *The Greedy Cat* © 1978, 1983 Margaret Mayo; David Higham Associates Ltd for *Cats* by Eleanor Farjeon from THE CHILDREN'S BELLS published by Oxford University Press; Faber and Faber for *How the Cat Became* from HOW THE WHALE BECAME by Ted Hughes and for *The Old Gumbie Cat* from OLD POSSUM'S BOOK OF PRACTICAL CATS by T.S. Eliot; Methuen Children's Books for *First Drive in the Miaow-Major* from ALL ABOUT SEMOLINA SILKPAWS by Gladys Williams; Scolar Press for an abridgement of THE ISLE OF CATS by John Symonds.

Puss in Boots

There was once a miller who had three sons. When the miller died, he left them his windmill, his donkey and his cat. The eldest son had the windmill, the second the donkey and the youngest got the cat.

The youngest son was very sad: 'With the windmill and the donkey, my brothers will have no trouble in making a living. But I will starve to death.'

The cat heard this, and looking very grave and serious, said: 'Master, give me a sack, and have a pair of boots made for me, and you will see what I can do for you.'

His master could not believe this, but he knew the cat was clever at catching rats and mice, so he began to cheer up.

When the cat had got what he had asked for, he pulled on his boots and set off, with the sack over his shoulder.

After a while he came to a cornfield, where he hid himself among the corn, but he kept his sack open, and when two partridges went into the sack, he pulled tight the strings and caught them both. Then he set off to see the King.

On arrival at the palace the cat was taken to the King. He made a deep bow and said: 'Your Majesty, the Marquis of Carrabas begs you to accept this present.'

The King was very pleased with the partridges.

The cat continued to bring the King gifts of game for the next two or three months. Then one day, when the cat knew that the King was going for a drive along the river bank with his daughter, the most beautiful princess in the world, the cat said to his master: 'Do as I tell you and your fortune is made. Just bathe in the river at the place I show you, and leave the rest to me.'

The miller's son did as he was told. When the King's carriage came by, the cat cried out, 'Help! Help! The Marquis of Carrabas is drowning!' The King put his head out of the carriage window and, recognizing the cat, sent his footmen to rescue the Marquis. Then the cat told the King that thieves had stolen his master's clothes. The truth was that the cat had himself hidden them under a big stone. Immediately the King heard this, he ordered his footmen to fetch one of his best suits for the Marquis to wear.

The Marquis looked very handsome in his borrowed clothes, and the princess fell madly in love with him.

The King then asked the Marquis to join them, and the carriage continued on its way.

The cat, very pleased to see his plan already beginning to work, ran ahead. Meeting some men mowing a meadow, he said to them: 'If you do not tell the King that these meadows belong to the Marquis of Carrabas, you will be chopped up into pieces as small as mincemeat.'

And when the carriage passed by a moment later, and the King stopped to ask who owned the meadows, the men said the Marquis of Carrabas, for they were frightened by the cat's threats.

Then the cat, still running on ahead, met some harvesters. The cat said: 'If you do not tell the King that these cornfields belong to the Marquis of Carrabas, you will be chopped up into pieces as small as mincemeat.' And again, when the King came by a moment later and wanted to know who owned the cornfields, he received the same reply.

At last, the cat came to a beautiful castle surrounded by a deep moat. The castle belonged to a very rich Ogre, who was the real owner of the fields the cat had claimed for his master.

Boldly, the cat walked in and asked to speak to him.

The Ogre received him as politely as an Ogre can.

'I am told,' said the cat, 'that you are so clever you can turn yourself into any animal you wish – a lion or an elephant even?'

'But of course,' said the Ogre. 'I'll show you.'

And immediately, the Ogre turned into a lion.

The cat was so frightened to see a lion in front of him that he leapt onto the roof – but his boots were not meant for clinging to tiles and he nearly slipped off.

A little later, when the cat saw that the Ogre had changed back into his own shape again, he came down.

'I am also told,' said the cat, 'but I can hardly believe it, that you can turn yourself into something very small – a rat, or a mouse even?'

'Nothing could be easier,' said the Ogre. And he turned himself into a mouse and began to scamper across the floor.

Now the cat seized his chance and pounced on the mouse and ate it up.

Meanwhile, the King's carriage was passing the castle. The King thought it was such a beautiful castle he must see inside. As soon as the cat heard the noise of the carriage passing over the drawbridge, he ran outside to meet it.

'Welcome to the castle of the Marquis of Carrabas, Your Majesty,' said the cat.

'What?' cried the King. 'Is this castle yours also, Marquis? May we go inside?'

Then the King, and the Marquis with the young princess on his arm, followed the cat into the castle.

They found themselves in a great hall with a marvellous feast spread out before them.

After the King had refreshed himself with good food and wine, he asked the Marquis, 'Would you do me the honour of marrying my daughter?'

The Marquis was only too happy to accept and he married the princess that very day.

As for the cat, he was made a great Lord, and no longer chased mice, except to amuse himself.

Charles Perrault

There lived an old man in a garret,
  So afraid of a little tom-cat,
That he pulled himself up to the ceiling,
  And hung himself up in his hat.

D'Arcy Wentworth Thompson

I'm not frightened of Pussy Cats,
They only eat up mice and rats,
But a Hippopotamus
Could eat the Lotofus!

Spike Milligan

Gobbolino's Hallowe'en

Gobbolino the witch's cat had found a home at last with the kind farmer and his wife and their friendly children.

There was only one animal on the farm who was not his friend, and that was Noggins, the old black horse who was the farmer's pride and joy. The horse did half the work on the farm, and the farmer often said he could not manage without him. But Noggins took no notice at all of Gobbolino, and the little cat felt strangely shy in his company.

This was very unfortunate because they had to share a stable at night. The farmer's wife thought even kitchen cats were better sleeping out of doors.

Summer passed by, with hay-time and harvest, and then it was Hallowe'en. The black horse had been strangely restless all day long, and much to Gobbolino's surprise he began a conversation when the farmer had shut them into the stable at night.

'Little Gobbolino! Do you know what day it is?'

'Oh yes, I do! It's Hallowe'en!' said Gobbolino, happy to be safely indoors on such an evening.

'Gobbolino! Are the stars shining? Is the moon full?' asked the horse.

'Yes it is, it is! The moon is full and the stars are shining!' said Gobbolino.

'Open the stable door so I can see the moon and the stars!' said the black horse.

Gobbolino did not dare to open the full stable door in case the horse should get out. But he opened the top half with his paw. The black horse whinnied with excitement.

'Gobbolino! Do you know who I really am?' said the black horse.

'No!' said Gobbolino, frightened by the horse's flashing eyes and stamping hooves.

'Jump on my back, and I will tell you!' said the black horse mysteriously.

Gobbolino did not want to jump on his back, but he was afraid of offending the horse, so he did as he was told. Immediately the horse gave a whinney that was more like the whine of the wind.

'I am . . . A BROOMSTICK!' he yelled, and cleared the half-door of the stable at a bound; out, out into the night sky, with Gobbolino clinging to the shaft and begging him piteously to return.

'What will your master do without you?' wailed

16

Gobbolino, 'He has been good and kind to you all
your life, how can you treat him so? And all I want to
be is a kitchen cat! Oh why couldn't you leave me at
home?'

'Never fear, little Gobbolino!' sang the broomstick, 'By sunrise I shall be a horse again! When Hallowe'en is over I must be back in my stable or else I'll be a broomstick for ever and ever! Let's have fun, Gobbolino! Let's enjoy ourselves while it lasts!'

At these words Gobbolino's heart leapt in relief, and he began actually to enjoy the ride. It was a long while since he had ridden on a broomstick, and the last time he had been terribly frightened. Now he joined in the horse's wild delight, and mewed with excitement as they swooped between the stars.

But all of a sudden he called out: 'Noggins! Noggins! I can hear voices behind us! I can see broomsticks! We are being chased by witches!'

It was quite true. Gaining on them fast were half a dozen hideous witches, crying out:

'A broomstick! A broomstick and a cat! We'll have them! Catch them! Catch them!'

The broomstick doubled its speed. Gobbolino lay crouched on the shaft, his ears pressed close to his head. They flew across the valley at a tremendous speed, and up the sides of the Hurricane Mountains with the witches shrieking close on their tails. Half way up the peaks there was a goatherd's shed, and into this the broomstick hurled itself, hoping to escape from the flying hags behind them.

But the witches had seen his trick, and the next moment they were all at the door, looking inside, and pointing with their long, skinny fingers as they jeered in chorus: 'That's no true broomstick! That's old

Noggins from the farm! And that's no witch's cat! It's just a common little kitchen cat! Come away, sisters! Bang the door on them and come up over the mountain! Hallowe'en will soon be over!'

The witches disappeared in a chorus of screams. The door was slammed shut. Although Gobbolino scratched and the broomstick kicked they could not open it. Hour after hour went by and the witches did not return.

'I am finished!' said the broomstick in despair, 'I shall never get home before sunrise! And what use shall I be to my master if I stay a broomstick all my life?'

Gobbolino lifted up his voice in a despairing mew that could be heard at the top of the mountain. It was heard by the little mice that knew him as a kitten in the witch's cave where he had been born. He had always been kind to them and not teased them as his sister Sootica had done.

'That is Gobbolino the witch's cat!' said the mice, and they left the cave to go and see what was making him sound so sad.

Down the mountain pattered dozens and dozens of little feet, as one behind the other mice travelled the path, till they came to the goatherd's shed. Gobbolino saw them coming, through a chink in the door.

'Oh little mice! Little mice!' he cried joyfully, 'Please make a hole for us in the door, so my friend the

20

broomstick and I can escape from this hut! The witches have shut us up inside, and we have to get home before the sun rises!'

There was a pale glow now in the eastern sky. The sun would soon be climbing over the top of the mountain.

The mice set to work with a will. Soon the grinding and snapping of hundreds of mouse teeth made the splinters fly, and a round hole appeared in the door. Gobbolino squeezed himself through in a minute, but it took quite an effort for the broomstick to force its last bristles through the space, and now the sky was the colour of ripe apricots.

Crying their thanks to the mice, Gobbolino and the broomstick raced for home. The valley slipped away beneath them. The long blue dawn-shadows of the

mountains reached out their fingers to touch them and then fled away backwards as the sun rose.

The first beams chased them into the farmyard just as the black horse clattered across the cobblestones on iron-clad feet.

'Why, however did that horse get out?' the farmer cried in surprise, looking out of the window, 'And there's our little Gobbolino riding on his back for all the world as if he has brought him home again! I never thought those two had much to say to each other!'

But Gobbolino and the black horse had a secret now, to share, and they were friends for ever and ever.

Ursula Moray Williams

The Cat and the Mouse

There was once a cat who had lost her spectacles, and she simply couldn't settle down quietly by the fire until she had found them. She hunted high and she hunted low, she miaowed here and she miaowed there, and poked her nose into all the most unlikely places; but she couldn't find them.

'I know I had them on when I was drinking my milk,' she said, 'but I *can't* remember whether or not I had them, the last time I went out in the garden!'

Now, what had really happened is this. The cat had taken them off while she was washing her face, and had left them lying on the floor. Then she had dozed off to sleep, and a cheeky little mouse had come out of his hole. He was a bold little fellow, and very hungry; so

23

when he saw the cat was asleep, he took his chance and
crept out into the room to look for some crumbs to eat.
He did not find any crumbs, but he did find the cat's
spectacles, under the table.

'Ha, ha!' he thought. 'This is where I win!' and
seizing the spectacles, he raced back to his hole with
them.

When the other mice heard what he had done, they
were very glad and praised him a lot, and told him
how clever he had been. 'And now,' they said, 'she
won't be able to see to catch us!'

Meanwhile, the cat had at last made up her mind that
she could not find them, and she had better just go to
sleep and forget about them – and hope they would
find themselves. But the cocky little mice poked their
heads out of their holes and waggled their whiskers
with laughing to think how they had got the better of
the cat.

'Aha!' they squeaked to each other. 'Now she can't catch us!'

Cats never sleep very deep, and nothing wakes them so quickly as a mouse's squeak. The cat woke up at once. But cats are clever, and pussy was not going to show that she was awake. She just lay there with her eyes shut, listening to all they said.

'Ho, ho!' they said; and then they began to sing:

> *Ha-ha! Ho-ho! He-he!*
> *Pussy's lost her spectacles and so she can't see!*

Some of the mice had come out into the room and were actually dancing quite near to her. Then the cat pretended to wake up and be terribly worried.

'Oh dear!' she said. 'I can smell mice, but without my spectacles I can't see a thing!'

The mice scuttled off to a safe distance to watch her.

'I believe there is one over there,' she said, and pretended to make a clumsy pounce into the coal-scuttle, although she knew very well there was no mouse there at all. And then she actually bumped her head (on purpose) against the table-leg.

At that the mice were quite sure that she was almost blind without her spectacles, and became more cheeky than ever. They held hands and started dancing the Lambeth Walk all over the floor, teasing the poor cat and singing their silly song:

> *Ha-ha! Ho-ho! He-he!*
> *Pussy's lost her spectacles, and so she can't see!*
> *Pussy's lost her spectacles, and can't catch me!*

25

Meanwhile the clever cat still pretended to be nearly blind. The children's shoes were drying by the fire. She pretended to think that they were mice, and stalked them carefully, and then pounced. She actually picked up one of the shoes in her mouth and started to worry it. All the mice shouted with laughter. But the cat didn't drop the shoe: she ran round the room with it in her mouth. Then she dropped it right in front of the mouse-hole, so it blocked the door!

'Grrr!' she said in a growling voice. 'I'm blind, am I?'
And before they could collect their scattered little mousy wits, she pounced on one of them and gobbled him up. For the truth was that she only needed her spectacles for reading, and, in fact, she could see very well indeed without them!
The mice squeaked and the mice jibbered. They bolted this way and that on their nimble feet, but they could not get away from pussy – and before long she

had had the biggest meal of mice she had ever had in her life.

Presently only one of them was left; and that was the cheeky little mouse who had stolen her spectacles in the first place. He alone did not seem frightened. He did not try to run away; he just stood in the middle of the floor and waited.

'All right,' he said, 'but you had better not gobble *me!*'

The cat pounced and held him down with one paw.

'And why shouldn't I gobble *you?*' she said.

'Because,' said the mouse, 'if you do, you will never get your spectacles back at all. I am the only living person who knows where they are.'

The cat had not thought of that, and of course it was true.

'Will you promise not to gobble me if I give them back?' said the mouse.

'I will promise,' said the cat, 'not to gobble you now.'

'That won't do,' said the mouse. 'You artful thing! You must promise not to gobble me *ever*, or else I know you will have no mercy once you get your glasses back!'

By this time the cat was so full of mouse that one more or less did not matter much. Besides, she really did want her spectacles, for as well as reading, she needed them for fine sewing.

'All right,' she said, 'I promise not to gobble you ever. But you must promise, if I let you go, to bring them back to me.'

'I will,' said the mouse.

'Hand on your heart?' said the cat.

'Hand on my heart,' said the mouse, 'if you will let me get up to put it there.'

So the cat and the mouse both promised each other, each with a paw on his heart; and then the cat moved the shoe, and the mouse ran down his hole and fetched the spectacles.

And that is why in my house there is only one mouse, but he is the sleekest and laziest and fattest mouse you ever saw. He is never frightened of anyone, and will often sit under the table catching the crumbs as you drop them while you are eating your tea. But after he has had so much that he can hardly walk, it is quite common to see him sit down to warm his little pink nose in front of the fire, side by side with his dear old friend pussy!

Richard Hughes

The Owl and the Pussy-Cat

The Owl and the Pussy-cat went to sea
  In a beautiful pea-green boat,
They took some honey, and plenty of money,
  Wrapped up in a five-pound note.
The Owl looked up to the stars above,
  And sang to a small guitar,
'O lovely Pussy! O Pussy, my love,
  What a beautiful Pussy you are,
    You are,
    You are!
  What a beautiful Pussy you are!'

Pussy said to the Owl, 'You elegant fowl!
  How charmingly sweet you sing!
O let us be married! too long we have tarried:
  But what shall we do for a ring?'
They sailed away, for a year and a day,
  To the land where the Bong-tree grows,
And there in a wood a Piggy-wig stood
  With a ring at the end of his nose,
    His nose,
    His nose,
  With a ring at the end of his nose.

'Dear Pig, are you willing to sell for one shilling
    Your ring?' Said the Piggy, 'I will.'
So they took it away, and were married next day
    By the Turkey who lives on the hill.
They dined on mince, and slices of quince,
    Which they ate with a runcible spoon;
And hand in hand, on the edge of the sand,
    They danced by the light of the moon,
        The moon,
        The moon,
    They danced by the light of the moon.

Edward Lear

Why the Manx Cat Has No Tail

On the Isle of Man there live hundreds of cats that have no tails – no, nothing at all where a tail ought to be. And if you asked one of those Manx cats why he had no tail, he would tell you that it was because of a stubborn cat who was his mother's, grandmother's, grandmother's . . . grandmother's . . . and so on and on . . . way back to the time of Noah.

And here is how it happened.

Years and years ago Noah built an Ark. He built it large and he built it strong, because Noah knew that one day the rains would fall and the whole world would be flooded. When the Ark was finished, he called to the animals; and, two by two, they came. Day after day, week after week, Noah called. And still they came: large animals and small animals, fat animals and thin animals. And Noah and his wife and his sons found room for them all.

Now Noah himself had a cat that was a family pet. She was a sort of coppery colour, with big, round eyes, a very soft coat and a long and lovely tail. She was an affectionate cat, but she was stubborn, as stubborn as – well, as stubborn as only some cats can be.

The very morning the rains began to fall that cat decided to go out a-mousing. Other cats might hate the rain, but she did not care about a few drops of water. She wanted to go mousing and go mousing she would, even if it were the last thing she did. And it very nearly was!

The rains fell and they fell. It was the kind of morning that no self-respecting mouse would think to venture abroad. So though that copper-coloured cat was a fine mouser, she had no luck at all. But she went on trying.

Still the rains fell and they fell; and then, suddenly, the skies opened and it simply torrented down.

Noah looked out and saw the rains torrenting down, and he began to think that it was time he closed the door of the Ark. And then he saw that copper-coloured cat, the family pet, creeping about outside.

'Puss! Puss! Puss!' he called. 'Come, puss!'

And she heard all right. But what did she do? She waved her tail, careless like, and said to herself, 'I'll catch a mouse this day if it's the last thing I do.'

'Puss! Puss! Puss!' he called again. 'Come now, puss!'

And again she waved her tail, careless like.

'Time to close the door,' said Noah, shaking his head. And then in a loud voice, he cried out, 'Who's out is out and who's in is in!'

This time that cat turned and looked. Oh dear! – there was water lapping up against the foot of the Ark. And oh dear! – there was Noah, closing the huge, heavy door.

Then she was up and off, bounding towards the Ark, running for her life. But that door was slowly, slowly swinging shut . . . almost . . . almost . . . almost . . . Then – *whoosh*! – she squeezed herself through the merest crack.

Just in time? No, not quite. For as she came in Noah slammed the door shut, and oh! but it cut off her long and lovely tail.

But she *was* in. So she counted her blessings and sat down, wet through, quite bedraggled and all sore where her tail had been. And there and then she vowed that she would never, never go out in the rain again if she could help it.

Well, the rains fell for forty days and forty nights, and the whole world was flooded. But the Ark floated on the water; and Noah and his family and the animals and the copper-coloured cat were safe inside the Ark. And as time passed, her sore place healed.

After many months the flood subsided and the Ark settled on dry ground. And still the cat counted her blessings. But, there was no denying it, she *did* miss her tail.

Now how she had heard of the Isle of Man, I do not know. But as soon as the Ark had settled on dry ground that stubborn, copper-coloured cat said:

> *'Bee bo bend it,*
> *My tail's ended;*
> *But I'll go to Man,*
> *As fast as I can,*
> *And get copper nails*
> *And mend it.'*

And away she went and travelled the world until she came to the Isle of Man.

But she never did find copper nails nor her lost tail, so she never did mend it. And that is why, to this day, Manx cats have no tails and, of course, like every other cat, they truly hate the rain.

Margaret Mayo

How the Cat Became

Cat was a real oddity. The others didn't know what to make of him at all.

He lived in a hollow tree in the wood. Every night, when the rest of the creatures were sound asleep, he retired to the depths of his tree – then such sounds, such screechings, yowlings, wailings! The bats that slept upside-down all day long in the hollows of the tree branches awoke with a start and fled with their wing-tips stuffed into their ears. It seemed to them that Cat was having the worst nightmares ever – ten at a time.

But no. Cat was tuning his violin.

If only you could have seen him! Curled in the warm smooth hollow of his tree, gazing up through the hole at the top of the trunk, smiling at the stars, winking at the moon – his violin tucked under his chin. Ah, Cat was a happy one.

And all night long he sat there composing his tunes.

Now the creatures didn't like this at all. They saw no use in his music, it made no food, it built no nest, it didn't even keep him warm. And the way Cat lounged around all day, sleeping in the sun, was just more than they could stand.

'He's a bad example,' said Beaver, 'he never does a stroke of work! What if our children think they can live as idly as he does?'

'It's time,' said Weasel, 'that Cat had a job like everybody else in the world.'

So the creatures of the wood formed a Committee to persuade Cat to take a job.

Jay, Magpie, and Parrot went along at dawn and sat in the topmost twigs of Cat's old tree. As soon as Cat poked his head out, they all began together:

'You've got to get a job. Get a job! Get a job!'

That was only the beginning of it. All day long, everywhere he went, those birds were at him:

'Get a job! Get a job!'

And try as he would, Cat could not get a wink of sleep.

That night he went back to his tree early. He was far

too tired to practise on his violin and fell asleep in a few minutes.

Next morning, when he poked his head out of the tree at first light, the three birds of the Committee were there again, loud as ever:

'Get a job!'

Cat ducked back down into his tree and began to think.

He wasn't going to start grubbing around in the wet woods all day, as they wanted him to. Oh no. He wouldn't have any time to play his violin if he did that.

There was only one thing to do and he did it.

He tucked his violin under his arm and suddenly jumped out at the top of the tree and set off through the woods at a run. Behind him, shouting and calling, came Jay, Magpie, and Parrot.

Other creatures that were about their daily work in the undergrowth looked up when Cat ran past. No one had ever seen Cat run before.

'Cat's up to something,' they called to each other. 'Maybe he's going to get a job at last.'

Deer, Wild Boar, Bear, Ferret, Mongoose, Porcupine, and a cloud of birds set off after Cat to see where he was going.

After a great deal of running they came to the edge of the forest. There they stopped. As they peered through the leaves they looked sideways at each other and trembled. Ahead of them, across an open field covered with haycocks, was Man's farm.

But Cat wasn't afraid. He went straight on, over the field, and up to Man's door. He raised his paw and banged as hard as he could in the middle of the door.

Man was so surprised to see Cat that at first he just stood, eyes wide, mouth open. No creature ever dared to come on to his fields, let alone knock at his door. Cat spoke first.

'I've come for a job,' he said.

'A job?' asked Man, hardly able to believe his ears.

'Work,' said Cat. 'I want to earn my living.'

Man looked him up and down, then saw his long claws.

'You look as if you'd make a fine rat-catcher,' said Man.

Cat was surprised to hear that. He wondered what it was about him that made him look like a rat-catcher. Still, he wasn't going to miss the chance of a job. So he stuck out his chest and said: 'Been doing it for years.'

'Well then, I've a job for you,' said Man. 'My farm's swarming with rats and mice. They're in my haystacks, they're in my corn sacks, and they're all over the pantry.'

So before Cat knew where he was, he had been signed on as a Rat-and-Mouse-Catcher. His pay was milk, and meat, and a place at the fireside. He slept all day and worked all night.

At first he had a terrible time. The rats pulled his tail, the mice nipped his ears. They climbed on to rafters above him and dropped down – thump! on to him in the dark. They teased the life out of him.

But Cat was a quick learner. At the end of the week, he could lay out a dozen rats and twice as many mice within half an hour. If he'd gone on laying them out all night there would pretty soon have been none left, and Cat would have been out of a job. So he just caught a few each night – in the first ten minutes or so. Then he retired into the barn and played his violin till morning. This was just the job he had been looking for.

Man was delighted with him. And Mrs Man thought he was beautiful. She took him on to her lap and stroked him for hours on end. What a life! thought Cat. If only those silly creatures in the dripping wet woods could see him now!

Well, when the other farmers saw what a fine rat-and-mouse-catcher Cat was, they all wanted cats too. Soon there were so many cats that our Cat decided to form a string band. Oh yes, they were all great violinists. Every night, after making one pile of rats and another of mice, each cat left his farm and was away over the fields to a little dark spinney.

Then what tunes! All night long . . .

Pretty soon lady cats began to arrive. Now, every night, instead of just music, there was dancing too.

44

And what dances! If only you could have crept up there and peeped into the glade from behind a tree and seen the cats dancing – the glossy furred ladies and the tomcats, some pearly grey, some ginger red, and all with wonderful green flashing eyes. Up and down the glade, with the music flying out all over the night.

At dawn they hung their violins in the larch trees, dashed back to the farms, and pretended they had been working all night among the rats and mice. They lapped their milk hungrily, stretched out at the fireside, and fell asleep with smiles on their faces.

Ted Hughes

Rat a tat tat, who is that?
Only grandma's pussy cat.
What do you want?
A pint of milk.
Where's your money?
In my pocket.
Where's your pocket?
I forgot it.
Oh, you silly pussy cat!

Pussicat, wussicat, with a white foot,
When is your wedding and I'll come to it.
The beer's to brew, the bread's to bake.
Pussycat, pussycat, don't be too late.

Semolina Silkpaws' First Drive in the Miaow-Major

How wonderful it was for the kittens to go spinning down Catstown High Street in their very own motor car. Semolina, of course, made the Brigadier stop and change places directly they got outside the Orphanage gates. The kittens nearly burst with pride as they watched her settle herself in the driving seat and take the wheel between her paws.

'Look! She's driving it herself,' whispered the lady cats. 'Isn't she wonderful!'

'We hope our wives won't all start wanting to drive,' growled the gentlemen cats anxiously, as the Miaow-Major went spanking cheerfully along.

Down the road it sped, past the Town Hall where the Mayor and Aldermen leaned out of the windows, waving friendly paws. Faster still it went past Catstown Market where Mrs Whitefoot sat selling balloons.

Then even faster still the Miaow-Major flashed past

the *Catstown Companion* offices, where all the printer cats stopped printing to stand and cheer. And fastest of all it sped past Catstown Police Station, where P.C. Flatpaws looked and scratched his head and said, 'Now what was it Sergeant Sardine said about not going too fast? Why, she must be doing ninety miles an hour. Surely that's not allowed in Catstown!'

And at that very moment out from the corner where they had been hiding nosed the dread of every Catstown driver cat: the Speed Cops in their car, ready to chase and gong and stop and take off to prison any cat that they found going too fast.

49

'Oo-oo-oo-oh!' shivered the lady cats, and the Brigadier, glancing in the driving mirror and seeing the Speed Cops hurrying up behind, said anxiously, 'I think, dear Mrs Silkpaws, you ought to put the brake on.'

'Perhaps I ought,' said Mrs Silkpaws pleasantly, 'but I'm not quite sure which pedal that one is.'

'Wow-ow!' cried the kittens as the Miaow-Major shot forward faster still, right across the pavement towards the gleaming plate-glass window of Messrs Fin and Fur, proprietors of the Catstown Super-Fish Market.

'Aw-aw-aw-awgh!' gasped the Brigadier shakily. 'That wasn't the brake you put your paw on. That was the accelerator – the pedal that makes it go faster!'

So perhaps it was rather lucky for Semolina that a low, badly brought up cat (Mrs Whitefoot's second cousin) chose that very minute to come sneaking through the crowds carrying a large brick.

Slipping nippily between the Miaow-Major and the Super-Fish Market window, he flung his brick right through the plate-glass and thrust in a hairy paw after it. Seizing the most succulent pair of kippers, he made off with them down Catstown High Street.

'Oo-oo-oh, she's broken a window and the Speed Cops are after her,' cried a nervous cat, confused by the noise and excitement, and this disturbing news spread through the crowd.

'We might have known it,' said the gentlemen cats. But Semolina, neatly backing the car out of the shattered window, shot off after the disappearing smash-and-grab cat.

'Isn't this exciting,' cried the kittens. 'Just like television.'

Faster went the smash-and-grab cat. Faster still went Mrs Silkpaws. And fastest of all came the Speed Cops sounding their gong for all they were worth. All Catstown held its breath.

What a moment it was when suddenly Mrs Silkpaws swung the Miaow-Major round, and, at a slow, dignified crawl, returned towards Catstown Police Station with the smash-and-grab cat lying helpless across the bonnet, one ear firmly gripped by a stern-faced Brigadier, the cat's guilty paws still clutching the stolen kippers.

'So that's who broke the window,' said the watching lady cats.

'So that's why she was going so fast,' said the Speed Cops. 'That makes all the difference.'

'Attacat!' yelled the printer cats, leaning so far out of the windows of the *Catstown Companion* that they nearly fell out.

'Back to work!' roared the Editor. 'We'll print a special edition with big headlines, *Mrs Silkpaws Does It Again! Catstown Underworld Foiled*. It'll sell like hot cakes.'

The fish-shop cat pressed one of the kippers back into her gentle paws.

'Permit me, Madam,' he begged. 'Just a small mark of my gratitude and admiration.'

'Very nice of you, I'm sure,' said Mrs Silkpaws, 'but it's these kittens I'm worried about. They'll be late for school.'

'That would never do,' cried Sergeant Sardine, bustling up. Neatly flicking open the door of the Speed Cops' car she said, 'Jump in here, my dears. My pals will soon get you there. Nobody's going to gong them for going too fast.'

'Won't our teacher be surprised,' said the kittens delightedly. 'Aren't we lucky! Isn't Mamma wonderful!'

Gladys Williams

The Greedy Cat

There was a time when the cat and the parrot were friends; and they were such good friends that they agreed to have dinner together every day. One day the parrot was to invite the cat, and the next day the cat was to invite the parrot and so on, turn and turn about.

The cat's turn came first. So she went to market and bought a few grains of rice, a few grains of sugar and not more than a mouthful of milk. That was all.

And when the parrot came to dinner, there was the rice and the sugar and the milk laid out, waiting to be cooked. And who cooked it? Why, the parrot did. And when this meagre meal was ready, they shared it between them, half for one and half for the other.

The next day it was the parrot's turn. So he went to market and bought a sackful of flour, oodles of butter, bags of sugar and all sorts of other flavoursome things. Then home he came and mixed everything together and made some cakes. And he made enough cakes to fill

54

a washer-woman's basket – exactly five hundred little cakes.

When the cat came to dinner, the parrot piled up four hundred and ninety-eight cakes in front of her and kept only two for himself.

And the cat ate up the four hundred and ninety-eight cakes in three minutes and then said, 'I want some more.'

So the parrot gave her the two little cakes he had kept for himself.

And the cat ate them and then said, 'I want some more.'

'There are no more cakes,' said the parrot. 'But if you are still hungry, you may eat me.'

And the cat was still hungry, so she ate the parrot, bones, beak and feathers!

Just then an old woman chanced to pass by and she saw the cat eat the parrot and she was angry. She picked up a stone and shouted at the cat: 'Shoo! Shoo! Away with you, or I'll throw this stone.'

But the cat said, 'I have eaten five hundred cakes; I have eaten my friend the parrot; so shall I blush to eat this cross old woman? No, surely not.'

So – gobble, gobble, slip, slop – the cat ate the old woman.

Then the cat went walking along the road until she met a man with a donkey.

'Out of my way, cat,' said the man, 'or my donkey will kick you to pieces!'

But the cat said, 'I have eaten five hundred cakes; I have eaten my friend the parrot; I have eaten the cross old woman; so shall I blush to eat this foolish man and his donkey? No, surely not.'

So – gobble, gobble, slip, slop – the cat ate the man and his donkey.

Then the cat went walking along the road until she met a royal wedding procession. There was the king and his bride, and a fine company of soldiers, marching four by four, and a troop of elephants, walking two by two.

'Out of my way, cat,' said the king, 'or my elephants will trample you to death!'

But the cat said, 'I have eaten five hundred cakes; I have eaten my friend the parrot; I have eaten the cross old woman; I have eaten the foolish man and his donkey; so shall I blush to eat this king and his procession? No, surely not.'

So – gobble, gobble, slip, slop – the cat ate the king and his bride and the soldiers, marching four by four, and the elephants walking two by two.

Then the cat went on until she met a pair of land crabs.

'Run away, pussy-cat,' said the land crabs, 'or we will nip you.'

'Ha! ha! ha!' laughed the cat, shaking her fat sides. And they *were* fat by this time. 'I have eaten five hundred cakes; I have eaten my friend the parrot; I have eaten the cross old woman; I have eaten the foolish man and his donkey; I have eaten the king and his procession; so shall I run away from two land crabs? Not so. I will eat them also.'

And she pounced on the land crabs, and – gobble, gobble, slip, slop – in two swallows, down they went.

When the land crabs slid down the cat's gullet, they found themselves amongst a whole crowd of other creatures. There was the king sitting with his head in his hands; there was the king's new bride, lying down in a dead faint; there were the soldiers, trying to form into fours; there were the elephants, trumpeting loudly; there was the donkey braying and the man beating him with a stick; there was the parrot, sharpening his beak on his own claws; there was the old woman, shouting abuse at everyone; and, last of all, there were five hundred cakes, neatly piled in a corner.

Now the land crabs ran about to see what they could find; and they found that the inside of the cat was quite soft. So they opened their claws and – nip!snip! – they began to cut a hole. And – nip!snip! – they went on cutting until they had cut a big round hole.

Then out walked the land crabs and scuttled away, as fast as they could. Then out walked the king, carrying his bride; out walked the elephants, two by two; out marched the soldiers, four by four, out walked the old woman, giving the cat a right good piece of her mind; and, last of all, out came the parrot, with two little cakes, one in each claw.

And then they all went about their business as if nothing had happened. All that is but the cat, and she sat in the sun and quietly licked her wounds.

Margaret Mayo

Cats

Cats sleep
Anywhere,
Any table,
Any chair,
Top of piano,
Window-ledge,
In the middle,
On the edge,
Open drawer,
Empty shoe,
Anybody's
Lap will do,
Fitted in a
Cardboard box,
In the cupboard
With your frocks
Anywhere!
They don't care!
Cats sleep
Anywhere.

Eleanor Farjeon

The Old Gumbie Cat

I have a Gumbie Cat in mind, her name is
  Jennyanydots;
Her coat is of the tabby kind, with tiger stripes and
  leopard spots.
All day she sits upon the stair or on the steps or on
  the mat:
She sits and sits and sits and sits – and that's what
  makes a Gumbie Cat!

But when the day's hustle and bustle is done,
Then the Gumbie Cat's work is but hardly begun.
And when all the family's in bed and asleep,
She slips down the stairs to the basement to creep.
She is deeply concerned with the ways of the mice –
Their behaviour's not good and their manners not
    nice;
So when she has got them lined up on the matting,
She teaches them music, crocheting and tatting.

I have a Gumbie Cat in mind, her name is
    Jennyanydots;
Her equal would be hard to find, she likes the warm
    and sunny spots.
All day she sits beside the hearth or in the sun or
    on my hat:
She sits and sits and sits and sits – and that's what
    makes a Gumbie Cat!

But when the day's hustle and bustle is done,
Then the Gumbie Cat's work is but hardly begun.
As she finds that the mice will not ever keep quiet,
She is sure it is due to irregular diet
And believing that nothing is done without trying,
She sets straight to work with her baking and
    frying.
She makes them a mouse-cake of bread and dried
    peas,
And a *beautiful* fry of lean bacon and cheese.

I have a Gumbie Cat in mind, her name is
    Jennyanydots;
The curtain-cord she likes to wind, and tie it into
    sailor-knots.
She sits upon the window-sill, or anything that's
    smooth and flat:
She sits and sits and sits and sits – and that's what
    makes a Gumbie Cat!

But when the day's hustle and bustle is done,
Then the Gumbie Cat's work is but hardly begun.
She thinks that the cockroaches just need
     employment
To prevent them from idle and wanton destroyment.
So she's formed, from that lot of disorderly louts,
A troop of well-disciplined helpful boy-scouts,
With a purpose in life and a good deed to do –
And she's even created a Beetles' Tattoo.

So for Old Gumbie Cats let us now give three
     cheers –
On whom well-ordered households depend, it
     appears.

                                        T. S. Eliot

The Isle of Cats

Gabriel was just putting on his satchel, which was stuffed with books, a pencil-box and one ink-spattered exercise book, when he turned to his cat and said, 'Uncle Tom, I don't think I want to go to school today.'

Uncle Tom looked up and said, 'Well, don't go then.'

After this advice, he closed his eyes, yawned, arched his back and began to dig his claws in and out of the sofa. Uncle Tom was no ordinary cat, for he could tell the time, look through a telescope (keeping one paw over the other eye, of course), beat up an egg, steer a raft, smoke a pipe and do many other things.

'What shall I do instead?' asked Gabby (which is short for Gabriel), taking off his satchel. 'What are *you* going to do today?'

'Well, I'm going to see my grandmother,' said Uncle Tom. 'I received a letter from her some days ago, telling me she's not well.'

'I'm sorry to hear that,' said Gabby. 'And where does your grandmother live?'

'On the Isle of Cats,' replied Uncle Tom, twitching his ears, and flipping one of them with his paw.

'I wish you would take me with you,' said Gabby. 'Is it far away?'

'It is far away,' replied Uncle Tom; 'and the question is: can we get there and back by teatime?' He looked seriously at his wristwatch.

'Oh, do take me there, Uncle Tom,' cried Gabby; 'I don't mind if I am late for tea.'

'I do,' replied Uncle Tom; 'for there are shrimps for tea, and you know how much I like shrimps.'

67

They went into the garden together, and then Uncle Tom said, 'All right, I'll take you to the Isle of Cats. Jump on my back.'

Gabby was surprised at this, because Uncle Tom had never before offered to give him a ride on his back, but he did as he was told.

'Hold on tight,' said Uncle Tom, and with one bound he was over the garden wall and running so quickly down the lane that if Gabby hadn't held on tight, he would have fallen off.

A little while later, Gabby said, 'Oh, Uncle Tom, we *are* high up in the air, because a swan flew by me, and they always fly high, very high. And when I looked down I saw a church steeple. My head will soon touch the clouds.'

'Don't you know,' replied Uncle Tom, 'that all cats leap high when they're going to the Isle?'

'Dear Uncle Tom,' said Gabby after a while, 'I hope you'll bring me back safely.'

'Of course I will,' he replied.

At last Uncle Tom stopped leaping high.

'Are we there?' Gabby asked.

'Not quite,' said Uncle Tom.

Gabby looked round and saw they had arrived at the seashore. He slipped off Uncle Tom's back. 'Where's the Isle of Cats?' he said.

'Look,' said Uncle Tom, pointing.

Gabby looked and saw on the horizon an island with palm trees and, in the middle, a smoking volcano. 'There's the Isle of Cats,' said Uncle Tom.

A boat, rowed by six strong ginger cats, wearing sailor hats, three a side, was coming rapidly towards them. As soon as it arrived, one cat jumped ashore.

'It's all right,' said Uncle Tom, 'they will take us to the island.'

'But how did they know we were going to be here?' asked Gabby.

'Because,' said Uncle Tom, looking very pleased with himself, 'I sent them a postcard.'

'Ay, ay, sir,' said the Captain.

'Well, let's get in,' said Gabby impatiently. 'But I must say I've never before been rowed to an island by six ginger cats.'

'But they can row as fast as anyone, can't they?' said Uncle Tom.

Gabby had to agree, as he saw just how hard those ginger cats were rowing. Already he could make out a railway engine puffing its way round the island: it was being driven by two black cats, but whether they were black from the coal they kept shovelling into the furnace, or because their fur was black when they were born, he did not know.

They were soon rowed into the harbour and Gabby could see hundreds of cats: Black cats, White cats, Tabby cats, Ginger cats, Black *and* White cats, Siamese cats, Burmese cats; in fact, cats of all kinds. Some were peering at him through telescopes; and one rude cat,

Gabby noticed, snatched the telescope away from another cat to look through it himself.

'They find you very interesting,' said Uncle Tom. 'They've never seen a boy before.'

'Never seen a boy before?' said Gabby. 'Why that's absurd. Cats and boys are always together.'

'Not on this island,' said Uncle Tom. 'I'd better take you under my protection. I'll treat you as my pet.' And there and then he picked Gabby up as if he were a kitten and tucked him under his arm.

'Oh, do put me down, Uncle Tom,' said Gabby, kicking his legs in the air, 'you'll upset the boat. I'm not in the least afraid of all these silly cats, even if they are dressed up.'

'We cats,' said Uncle Tom proudly, 'like bright colours. My own waistcoat, for instance, is what you'd call sporting.'

For the first time Gabby noticed that Uncle Tom was wearing a red waistcoat and lemon-coloured gloves.

Suddenly tugs began to hoot, and a salute of three guns was fired from the beach by the Cat Fusiliers.

'What's that for?' asked Gabby.

'In honour of our visit, I should think,' said Uncle Tom.

'Well, if that's so,' replied Gabby, 'put me down so that I can be seen properly.'

'I must give these fellows something,' said Uncle Tom, putting Gabby down and taking out his purse.

'Here, buy a saucer of milk stout when you go

72

ashore,' he said, giving the sailor cats sixpence each. 'You'll need it: you've rowed so hard.'

As Gabby and Uncle Tom climbed up the harbour steps, a brass band began to play, and they found themselves being greeted by a very important-looking cat with a gold chain round his neck. 'Welcome to the Isle of Cats!' he said.

'Hurrah!' cried the crowd, throwing their hats and caps into the air: and all the kittens who had been let out of school to welcome Gabby and Uncle Tom, waved their flags furiously.

'Thank you,' said Gabby. 'Thank you with all my heart.'

'He's the Mayor,' whispered Uncle Tom to Gabby, 'so be nice to him.'

'I never expected this grand welcome,' said Gabby.

The Mayor replied, but what he said was drowned in a great blare from the trumpet.

'You're meant to take this,' said a little kitten in a pink silk dress, coming forward and giving Gabby a bunch of flowers.

'Hurrah!' shouted the crowd.

'Hurrah!' shouted Uncle Tom.

'Thank you,' said Gabby to the little kitten in the pink dress.

He was still saying thank-you as he and Uncle Tom were being driven away in the Mayor's car, followed by various cats on bicycles, tricycles and penny farthings.

'Where are we going to?' Gabby asked.

The Mayor took a piece of paper out of his pocket. 'Let me look at the programme,' he said, adjusting his spectacles. 'To the wrestling match first of all, then to the mouse-catching classes for orphan kittens.'

'I've got to see my grandmother,' said Uncle Tom. 'She's not well.'

'What's the matter with her?' asked the Mayor.

'She sees everything double,' said Uncle Tom.

'Then she'll see two of you, when you get there,' said the Mayor.

'That's right,' said Uncle Tom.

'Can you tell me,' asked the Mayor, 'which of you she'll speak to?'

'Which of us?' asked Uncle Tom. 'I don't know what you mean.'

'Well,' said the Mayor explaining, 'if she sees two of you, which of you will she speak to?'

While Uncle Tom was thinking out the answer, the Mayor said, 'Let's go to the wrestling match first: that will give your grandmother more time to recover.'

'Wrestling,' said Uncle Tom, 'is cats' favourite pastime.'

'Tim the Terror is wrestling with the Furry Fury,' explained the Mayor.

When they arrived, they found the match had already begun. Two big cats were wrestling in the centre (and sometimes on the edge) of the ring. The Furry Fury was a ginger cat with torn ears and a fearful growl. He was simply bulging with muscles. The celebrated Tim the Terror was a black cat with one tooth missing and gigantic paws. They were both stripped to the waist and above their heads hung a large notice which said:

NO SCRATCHING

The sound of the gong ended the 26th round.

The 27th round began with Tim the Terror leaping in the air and landing upon the Furry Fury. The Furry Fury was knocked over, but he did not wait to be jumped on again; he grabbed hold of the Terror's tail, pulled him down and rolled on top of him.

'Coo, can't those cats wrestle!' exclaimed Gabby. 'I've never seen anything like it.' Then Tim the Terror seized the arm of the Furry Fury in a half-nelson grip and had him over on his back before you could say 'fish!'

'A point to you!' shouted the referee who kept on skipping in and out of the ring in case he should be caught by one of the wrestlers in mistake for the other – they would close their eyes and rush at each other like rockets chasing the moon.

The crowd rose up with shrieks and hisses on hearing the referee give a point to the Terror, but whether this was because they agreed or disagreed, Gabby could not say.

'Looks as if Tim's going to win,' said the Mayor, offering Gabby a sweet.

'I've seen enough,' said Gabby.

'But they've hardly begun,' said the Mayor. 'They'll wrestle for hours yet.'

'I think the Furry Fury looks half-dead already,' said Gabby.

'Yes, he's finished,' said Uncle Tom.

The Terror had seized him by the tail and was swinging him round and round the ring.

Suddenly the Furry Fury, hissing like one of those improved steam-engines, shot up to the glass roof and with a loud crash, disappeared. You see, Tim the Terror had let go of his tail.

'Now,' said the Mayor, looking at the programme, 'we must go to the Hall of Fame.'

'I thought,' said Gabby, 'we were meant to see the orphan kittens next.'

'How about my grandmother?' asked Uncle Tom. 'I must go to see her. I've brought her a pair of spectacles.'

'To your grandmother,' said the Mayor, 'we shall go then.'

When they arrived, they found her in bed with a bandage round her head, looking very cross-eyed and angry.

'How did it happen?' Uncle Tom asked.

'A pot fell on my head,' she said, 'and I've seen double ever since.'

'How many of me do you see?' asked the Mayor.

'Two,' said Uncle Tom's grandmother.

'And how many of me?' asked Uncle Tom.

'Two!' she replied.

'And how many of me?' asked Gabby.

'Two!!' she cried.

'How many fingers and thumbs have I got?' asked
Gabby holding up his two hands.

'Twenty!!!' she screamed.

'What does the doctor say?' asked Uncle Tom.

'He says I'll never be better till I'm tossed in a
blanket, but I don't like that.'

'You are quite right,' said Uncle Tom. 'Try these instead.' And he took out of his pocket the spectacles he had brought for her.

The old lady in the bed put them on carefully and then began to smile. 'Half of you have gone,' she said.

'How many are there of me?' asked the Mayor.

'One,' she said.

'And of me?' asked Gabby.

'One,' she said.

'And of me?' asked Uncle Tom.

'One, only one.'

'Then you're cured,' said the Mayor.

'Yes, you are cured,' said Uncle Tom.

'Good-bye,' said Gabby. 'Don't let any more pots fall on your head.'

John Symonds